709

O9-BTO-287

To Zoe and her mother, Emily,
who share the wonderful world of story.   —J.C.

For my children, Cameron, Matthew and Georgia.   —E.F.

P a t r i c i a   L e e   G a u c h ,   E d i t o r

PHILOMEL BOOKS
A division of Penguin Young Readers Group.   Published by The Penguin Group.
Penguin Group (USA) Inc., 375 Hudson Street, New York, NY 10014, U.S.A.
Penguin Group (Canada), 10 Alcorn Avenue, Toronto, Ontario, Canada M4V 3B2 (a division of Pearson Penguin Canada Inc.)
Penguin Books Ltd, 80 Strand, London WC2R 0RL, England.
Penguin Ireland, 25 St. Stephen's Green, Dublin 2, Ireland (a division of Penguin Books Ltd.)
Penguin Group (Australia), 250 Camberwell Road, Camberwell, Victoria 3124, Australia (a division of Pearson Australia Group Pty Ltd).
Penguin Books India Pvt Ltd, 11 Community Centre, Panchsheel Park, New Delhi - 110 017, India.
Penguin Group (NZ), Cnr Airborne and Rosedale Roads, Albany, Auckland 1310, New Zealand (a division of Pearson New Zealand Ltd).
Penguin Books (South Africa) (Pty) Ltd, 24 Sturdee Avenue, Rosebank, Johannesburg 2196, South Africa.
Penguin Books Ltd, Registered Offices: 80 Strand, London WC2R 0RL, England.

Design by Semadar Megged.   Text set in 19-point AvantGarde Demi.   The art was done in watercolor and ink on watercolor paper.

Library of Congress Cataloging-in-Publication Data
Cowley, Joy.   Mrs. Wishy-Washy's Christmas / Joy Cowley ; illustrated by Elizabeth Fuller.   p. cm.
Summary: When Mrs. Wishy-Washy asks her farm animals to take a bath for Christmas, they find a way to take one without freezing.
[1. Domestic animals—Fiction. 2. Baths—Fiction. 3. Christmas—Fiction. 4. Stories in rhyme.] I. Fuller, Elizabeth (Elizabeth A.), ill. II. Title.
PZ8.3.C8345Mr 2005   [E]—dc22   2004015741   ISBN 0-399-24344-5
1 3 5 7 9 10 8 6 4 2
First Impression

Mrs. Wishy-Washy's Christmas

Joy Cowley   illustrated by **Elizabeth Fuller**

PHILOMEL BOOKS   •   NEW YORK

Snowflakes flew around
like big white bees,
and landed on the arms of winter trees.

Snow on the house. Snow on the farm.
Snow on the roof of the Wishy-Washy barn.

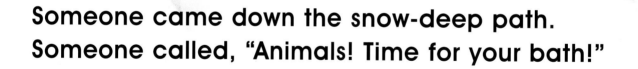

Someone came down the snow-deep path.
Someone called, "Animals! Time for your bath!"

The animals gasped.
They shivered and groaned.
"Not a cold bath!" the old cow moaned.

Mrs. Wishy-Washy filled the big tin tub.
"All get ready for your Christmas scrub!"

"I'm cold!" mooed the cow. "I'll get the flu!"
"I'm cold!" squealed the pig. "My snout is blue."
"I'm cold!" quacked the duck. "My feathers are ice.
I'm chilled to the bill and that's not nice."

"Oh, fiddle-dee-dee!" Mrs. Wishy-Washy said.
"Scrub yourselves from foot to head.
I'm going to town. When I get back,
you must be as clean as a brand-new tack.
No dirt, no mess, no mud, do you hear?
Or there'll be no presents for you this year."

Away she went in her old farm truck,
while the cow and the pig
and the shivering duck
stared at the ice in the old tin tub.
How could they sit in *that* for a scrub?

The cow mooed,
"No! I'll wheeze and sneeze!"
The pig squealed,
"No! My snout will freeze!"
The duck quacked,
"No! No way I can!
But don't worry, friends,
I have a plan."

So the cow and the pig left the ice-cold bath
and followed the duck up the Wishy-Washy path.
They squashed through the gate,

they squished through the door,
dripping mud and slush on the
Wishy-Washy floor.

"Come!" quacked the duck. "I'll show you the way to a bath as sweet as a hot summer day."

Oh, heaven! Oh, bliss! A wishy-washy place!
Shampoo for the hair and cream for the face.
Pink tub, pink towels, a little pink rug
and water as warm as a friendly hug.

They jumped right in with splashes and sploshes
and rose pink soap for their Christmas washes.
Oink, oink! Quack, quack! Moo, moo, moo!
they sang through the bubbles of the pink shampoo.

When Mrs. Wishy-Washy came back to the farm, she let out a scream like a fire alarm.

"Oh, my! Burglars! Just look at this mess!
Who was in my bathroom? Let me guess!"

There they were, by the Christmas tree,
the bathroom burglars, one, two, three,

shiny as tacks from heads to toes
and smelling as sweet as a new pink rose.

When they saw Mrs. Wishy-Washy, they gulped. Oh, my!
They could kiss their Christmas presents good-bye.

She would wag her finger and yell, "No, no!"
and send them back to their tub in the snow.

But Mrs. Wishy-Washy said,
"Fiddle-dee-dee!
I'm not as mad as I ought to be.
Cow, pig, duck, it's the time of year
for peace and happiness
and good cheer."

Then she put her Santa hat on her head
and gave them gifts wrapped in green and red.

The pig got bubble bath,
the duck got soap.
The cow got a brush
on the end of a rope.

Mrs. Wishy-Washy said with a little laugh,
"I'll put warm water in your old tin bath,
but don't use mine again, do you hear?
Merry Christmas and a Happy New Year."

Oink, oink! Quack, quack!
Moo, moo, moo!
Thank you, Mrs. Wishy-Washy!
Yes, Mrs. Wishy-Washy!
Dear Mrs. Wishy-Washy!
Merry Christmas to you, too!